For
My wife Lisa
And my daughters Ashley and Amanda
You are my world

Bella who lived in Branchville
Owned a very unique boutique
She sold all types of umbrellas
And always sold them cheap!

The many shelves were full
The umbrella racks as well
No matter what you're looking for
Just go in and ring the bell!

Umbrellas for the rain
Others for the snow
Umbrellas for hot sunny days
When you need one, who could know

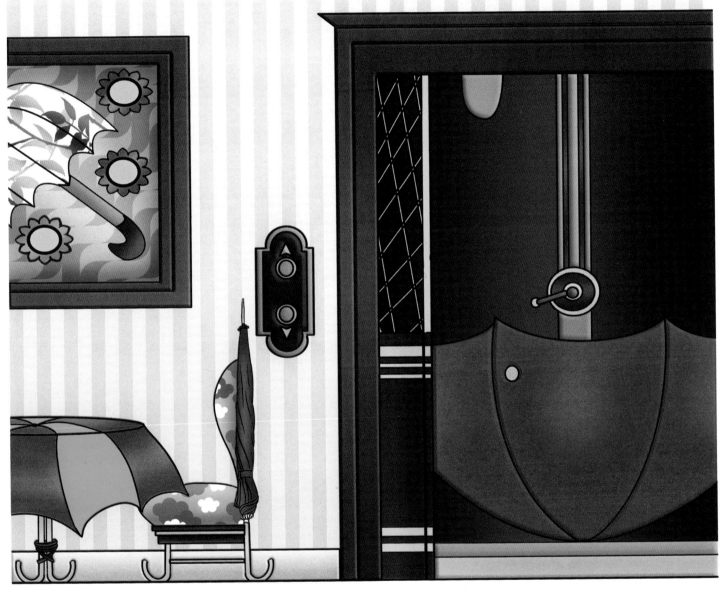

Her store is very different
With umbrellas as tables and chairs
To get up to the second floor
Use the umbrella elevator, not the stairs

Bella has so many colors
Her favorite one is, flamingo pink
One could never have too many umbrellas
She will tell you with a wink

Umbrellas made with colorful stripes
Others with polka dots
Umbrellas made all different ways
With a guarantee there's lots and lots!!
Red ones, bright yellow ones, purple,
orange, peach and blue
All colors of the rainbow
Bella is sure she has one for you

Bella's umbrellas are seen at ballparks

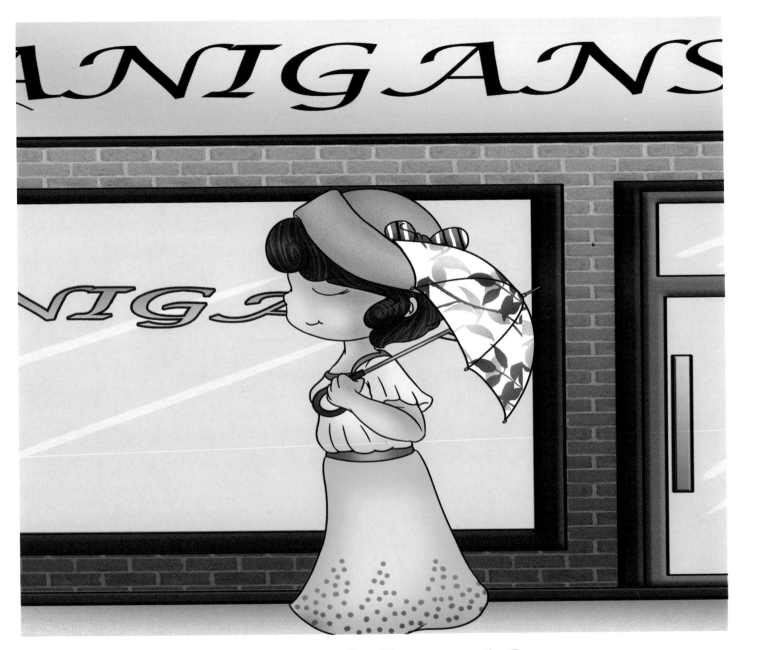

They are spotted all around the town

I have seen them on a big cruise ship

And at the movies lost and found!

One day a strange thing happened
The brakes on a train had failed
It was headed straight for the city
As the whistle wailed and wailed

As the news was quickly reported
About the danger just ahead
Bella knew this was a big problem
And thought while scratching her head

After thinking long and hard
Bella knew just what to do
She would use her special umbrellas
Then off to the boutique Bella flew

From the boutique, she phoned all her friends
And told them to come to her shop
They gathered all the umbrellas up
And all that was left was a mop

Bella's plan was very simple
They would line the railroad tracks
Each one holding out an umbrella
They took from the boutique's shelves and racks
Bella told her friends real calmly
To watch out for the speeding train
And only on her signal
Open the umbrellas, all the same

The speed was very fast
As the train approached the town
The passengers could clearly see
Lots of people all around

The train's whistle blew and blew
Its metal wheels were loud
As the train quickly approached
The anxious waiting crowd
Then at that very moment
Bella raised her shaking hand
She signaled to everyone present
To activate the plan

The train's conductor yelled: "Open all the windows
Hurry, everyone do it fast!
Reach out of all the windows
Take an umbrella in your grasp!"

Countless umbrellas snapped open
It was such an amazing sight!
Each was handed to a passenger
And told to, hold on tight!

The umbrellas caught the wind
As the train roared down the tracks
But the passengers held on tight
To the umbrellas and their hats

All colors shapes and sizes
What a beautiful sight to behold
Umbrellas covered most of the train
As the wheels continued to roll

Then just what Bella had hoped
The train began to slow down
Bella's plan was somehow working
As the train arrived in town
When the train approached the station
It came to a sudden stop!
The passengers and town were safe
And on time according to the clock!

The passengers all cheered
As they exited the train
The conductor was looking all around
As he called out Bella's name

He found her in the crowd
Making sure everyone was okay
He thanked Bella for all her help
And told her she saved the day

The crowd lifted Bella up on their shoulders
And carried her to the train
They placed her on the rear caboose
But Bella did not want all this fame

Bella thanked all that helped
And told them, it was really all of you
We all worked well together
The Wind, and my umbrellas too!
Bella then opened up an umbrella
Her favorite one, flamingo pink
You can never have too many umbrellas
She told the crowd with a smiling wink

Made in the USA
Lexington, KY
10 June 2013